COWBOYS' MEDICAL AGE GAP

Fertile First Time Story

Leandra Camilli

CONTENTS

Title Page

Copyright

Chapter 1   1

Chapter 2   5

Chapter 3   8

Chapter 4   11

Chapter 5   14

Sneak Peek: Cowboys' Lucky Age Gap   19

Books by this Author   21

About the Author   23

CHAPTER 1

"Hmmm, does this make you feel better?" The doctor asked, his straw hat lowering on his head. With devilish eyes, he made me feel a little uncomfortable as he groped me. He kept saying that I had pretty, big breasts, his fingers digging into my skin.

I had no idea how I was supposed to feel about this.

"Doctor, what are you doing?" I asked, remembering that soon I was going to start my job as a farmhand. I was in their farmhouse. The cowboys' farmhouse, to be more precise. They put me here to be with this doctor, and it was a bit disappointing. I thought that my first day on the farm was going to be a little more action-packed.

"Nothing out of the ordinary. Just making sure you're getting used to the changes..."

The changes. I remembered them. The cowboys' mentioned them, and then I agreed with them. And I had to say that what they mentioned was true and that it was happening. I could feel my body hotter. My breasts were getting bigger with every passing second.

And the nice doctor wasn't taking his hands off at all. If anything, he was digging his fingers further into the skin of my right breast. Something about the way he was doing it was turning me on, and I didn't know what it was. After checking out some hot guys on the web, I couldn't help but admit that he looked just like them.

Something about him made me feel hotter down there. I didn't know what it was, but it was originating there and traveling through my whole body. And the way the nice doctor kept applying pressure with his hands, too... He cranked up how desperate I was feeling about him. I wanted now, more than ever, to feel him inside me.

I wanted his fingers to move further down.

He didn't have a mask on, and I could see the dirty smile on his face widening.

"Do you like it when I move my hand like this, Linda?" He asked, drawing small circles on my skin. The way he was regarding me with his eyes, I could only nod at it. He widened his smile a little more, hairs on his arms poking out through the holes of his white coat. Looking a little beyond them, I could see several veins popping out on his forearms. He was a man with a perfect, defined body, I noticed.

"Good. Is it making you feel less pain?" He asked, moving his hand a little further down, until it was resting on my belly. Now he was making me feel an ounce of coldness I didn't know was even there. I didn't know what he was thinking about doing with me, but I could tell it wasn't anything innocent.

He was thinking about putting something inside me. What it was, I didn't know, but the way he was looking down at my hole – and I didn't even know what that other part of me was called – I could tell it. With absolute certainty, I could tell so.

"Yes, doctor," I responded, still feeling his hand on my belly. Making small circles on it, the nice doctor decided to move his hand even further down than it was before. Now, it was resting right where my hole was.

"What is that?" I asked him, not sure if I was making a mistake or not. I was curious. My body was hot, ripples of pleasure traveling through it. The longer this went on, the more I was beginning to wonder why I was naked. Perhaps it was something the doctor needed to do that was connected to me.

"It's something very special," he said, poking his finger against it. When he did that, he made me squirm. I felt a wave of pleasure through my body that emanated from there and moved through every cell of my body.

Beads of sweat pooling on my forehead, I could only wonder what was going on in his head.

"What do you mean 'special'?" I asked, pressing my legs together. Something about the way he was moving his hand and poking his finger against my flesh was making me feel exposed. I felt threatened and that I needed to protect myself.

"It means that it needs something inside it," Robert said, his other hand moving to where his crotch was. I could see something poking against his pants, making a shadow that resembled a shaft. I had no idea what it was, but it was between his legs and it looked pretty thick and big.

"What kind of thing?" I asked, warmth rushing to my cheeks.

The man chuckled, moving his finger so that it was beginning to get inside my hole.

"Something like this," the nice doctor said, pulling at his crotch. He made whatever was hiding behind his pants move up and down, a blotch of something wet spreading through the fabric.

"What is that?" I asked, remembering that I was 19 and still didn't know anything about dealing with men. There was just something about them that piqued my interest and made me wonder what they were like without their clothes on. As someone who didn't know much about sex and that sort of thing, I wondered what it even was like and how it worked. I was fully innocent, like a flower beginning to bloom.

"It's for you," he said, taking his hand out of my hole. When his fingers weren't pressing against my flesh anymore, I felt a little empty on the inside, like it was missing someone or something very important to me.

While I didn't know much about that, I did know that my body was getting hotter as the seconds passed. It was like every cell in it was beginning to resonate and act out of its own accord. It was as if I was starting to lose control of who I was.

The doctor snuck his fingers under his pants and started to lower them. The moment his pants were at his knees and I could see what his underwear was like, I lost consciousness. Darkness started to spread around my eyes and, in seconds, I was falling asleep.

I was falling asleep while the nice doctor was beginning to do something very nice and naughty to me.

CHAPTER 2

Opening my eyes, I thought I was going to feel the hands of the doctor moving over my body. But as the seconds passed and that didn't happen, I turned my head from left to right, taking in the environment. I was still in the same operation room, but now I noticed that my breasts were even bigger than before. It was like something was growing inside them.

Sighing, I realized I should have asked the doctor what was happening to me.

I didn't feel sore anywhere other than in my breasts. They were feeling so sore that it made me move my hand down, cupping my right breast. I applied pressure on the skin, and something white and a little frothy came out of it. It was milk. I was more surprised than anything, my eyes going wide.

Milk flowing over the wall and down to the floor, I heard the floor creaking as a pair of footsteps approached the door. As it creaked open, I turned my head in the direction the pair of footsteps came from.

I was surprised that it was still the nice doctor from before. I was even more surprised than usual because, this time, he was naked. Like when he was born, from top to bottom, the statue of a man who knew who he was.

And seeing him the way he was, it made me feel hotter and like I was running out of breath. He wrapped his fingers around the doorknob and closed the door, sealing me inside with him.

"Tell me, my little angel, are you surprised you are seeing me like this?" He asked, taking a step toward me while I could only look at what was between his legs. I had no idea what it was called, but it had such a strong presence it was like it was drawing me to him.

"I am..." I answered, my hand moving up out of its own accord. Seeing that, he smiled and wrapped his fingers around it. I tried to move it away from him right away, but he gripped it tightly and kept it in place.

"No, no, and no," he said, moving my hand so that it was touching the tip of whatever was between his legs. I just had no idea what it was called, being someone who grew up protected from everyone and everything.

Despite that, I was consenting to what was happening. There was just something about this man that was drawing me to him, that was making me want to have him inside of me.

"What are you going to do, doctor?" I asked, feeling my hole getting wetter as the seconds passed.

"Maybe this?" He said, scooting over so that he was right by my side and lowering his head until his lips were right above my nipple. Opening his mouth, he blew a cloud of hot air over it. It was enough to make me squirm and close my eyes, my body so hot I was wondering if I had a fever.

"That was so good, doctor," I said, my voice husky and throaty.

"Your breasts must be really sore right now," he said, his voice low as he started to wrap his lips around my nipple. The moment they were enclosed around it, it was like he was sending me to heaven. Everything was perfect, stars exploding in my vision, my breathing beginning to quicken.

"Yes, they are, doctor," I said, wishing he was inside of me, and I was surprised that sentence popped up in my mind like it was something I always knew about.

The doctor took his lips off my nipple for a fraction of a second, just to say, "You are so innocent and shy. It makes this even tastier."

"And what is it that we are doing?" I asked him, realizing he wasn't going to answer me because his lips were already back around my nipple. Applying enough pressure to get me going, he made me feel something surging through my body, ending right where my nipples were.

And moments later, my body was thrashing about. My vision started to darken and, as I thought I was going to fall asleep again, his other hand gripped my neck as he dug his fingers into my skin.

"Don't fall asleep just yet," he ordered, and I had to obey. "What you had is called an orgasm." As he finished saying that, his eyes locked with mine as I knew he was telling me a million things through them.

"It's so good," I said as his lips were already applying pressure on my nipple. And whatever he was doing to it, it was working. The milk was squirting out into his mouth, and I could see he was so hungry his throat's muscles were straining as he chugged down all of my milk.

Shaking my head, I was still surprised I was lactating. I guessed that the whole thing about becoming a hucow really was true, I thought to myself as I started to regain consciousness of my surroundings and the fact that the nice doctor was still keeping me all for himself.

For the time being. The door opened and in stepped a man who I knew well. The cowboy who owned this farm. He came to say hi.

CHAPTER 3

"Ah, Linda, how come you're already 19 and don't know anything about these things?" Otis murmured, his hand going for what was between his legs. It was thick, veiny, and pointing right at me. Feeling like something primitive inside of me was blowing up, I was already opening my mouth.

And he was climbing onto the medical bed. Crouching over me, he kept on stroking his shaft. I was going to keep calling it that from now on. I couldn't come up with a different term. While I didn't know much about sex, I knew that I wanted his shaft inside my mouth.

Otis was so willing to make that happen, too.

Looking a bit older than the doctor, he was everything I wanted right now. The doctor wasn't the kind of man to stay still and do nothing, too. He walked until he stood by the other side of the medical bed, lowering his head until his nose was right where my hole was. His fingers played with it, making small movements that sent ripples of pleasure through my whole body.

It was going to be just like that other time. He was going to make me feel again that thing called 'orgasm,' and it was going to be delicious. This being my first time doing it with two rough, dominating men, I couldn't help but feel afraid.

The nice doctor took his tongue out, flicking it over my cunt. Each flick sent shockwaves of pleasure through my body. I tried to moan, but something hard and meaty was already penetrating and filling it. Before long, I felt like I couldn't breathe.

"Fuck, she's so tight," Otis murmured more to himself than anyone. His hands roaming over my body, he started to roll his hips even as he was still crouched. It wasn't too long until he was picking up speed and I could feel his sack slapping against my chin.

I couldn't even move my tongue and please him the way he was doing to me. The way things were happening, it wasn't going to be too long until he was achieving his orgasm, too. While I didn't know much about sex, I was pretty sure he was going to achieve the same result I did. This man was going to be orgasming like I did.

Something about it also told me he wasn't going to be squirming like I did.

I tried breathing, even though it was the most difficult thing to be doing right now, while sweat collected all over my body. His dick was getting hotter, whatever was coming through his slit was lessening the friction, and his speed was even stronger than before.

I could hear sounds of our sex filling the room, and then he went still when his shaft started to throb. I knew that something was going to come out of it, just like my cunt spewed out juices all over the face of the doctor. I was just waiting for that to happen.

Arching my back, I felt like I was going to pass out when he started to unload whatever was in his sack. I was hoping that when we were finished, they would tell me everything about it too.

His stuff came out in hot ropes that started to fill up my mouth and throat. I had just about enough time to realize it was also very salty before feeling numb to everything else. Meanwhile, I could also feel the nice doctor's tongue lapping up my cunt juices. I was orgasming again, and I wasn't feeling ashamed of it.

He finished one last lick before looking up and into my eyes.

Widening his smile from between my legs, I knew that the nice doctor was far from being finished with me. "How are you feeling right now, Linda?" He asked, his hands moving over my legs as if he owned them.

"I don't think I can go on. I think I need a break," I responded, and he just waved his hand in dismissal.

"You'll get your break later." And as soon as he finished saying that, he lowered his head again and started to play with my slit using his tongue. Just like before, he slid it around slowly and carefully. The greed he was feeling right now was palpable. While Otis could do everything and anything he wanted with my mouth, my slit was for the doctor only.

His hands stopped moving for a moment, his fingers digging into my skin. Looking down, I could only wonder what he was planning on doing. In the meantime, Otis was pulling out of my mouth and moving his body so that his mouth was right where my boobs were. 'Boobs' was another term I learned about when I had sex for the first time.

And yes, I realized that meant I really lost that other thing they called my 'virginity.' I really needed to learn everything about sex so that every time I did this, I didn't feel like I was on an alien planet.

His finger drawing a small circle around my nipple, Otis asked, "Is this making you feel better?"

I could only nod, knowing that I didn't have another option. If I didn't do what the cowboy wanted, he would do worse things to me and I didn't want to disappoint him.

"Good to know that." And as soon as he finished saying that, he lowered his head again and wrapped his lips around my nipple. The first time I got milked, it was the doctor who did it for me, and now I was getting milked by the cowboy, too.

My vision darkening again, I knew that things were going to be even rougher than before.

CHAPTER 4

His lips applying pressure on my nipple, my body couldn't do anything that wasn't shooting out milk inside his mouth. Frothy and hot milk that was making him close his eyes in pleasure. The man was even making a *hmm* sound with his mouth that showed me how much he loved what he was tasting.

"It's delicious, isn't it?" The doctor asked, and I was so naïve and shy I wasn't even doing anything with my hands. In fact, my whole body was still, like their mere presence was paralyzing me.

Otis didn't respond to him, continuing what he was doing. I could feel his tongue applying pressure on my nipple, his hands moving over my shoulders as if he couldn't have enough of me. In the meantime, the nice doctor was rubbing a part of my slit that was making me feel even more pleasure than before. It was like I was submerged in a pool.

I could only close my eyes and take in what these guys were making me feel. I was the doctor's patient and also the cowboy's farmhand, and everything was perfect. And I could only wonder what holding one of those guys' shafts would be like. I was pretty sure I'd feel how hot they were, and also how hard.

Rubbing my clit even harder than before, it took the doctor no time at all to make me reach my orgasm again. Something about that word kept making me feel something was special about it, like it was going to lead me to learn new things about sex. Being 19 years old and already losing my virginity the way it was happening, I was going to have a lot of stories to tell my friends about.

"That's a bit too much," I tried telling them, but they weren't listening. The doctor started to rub my clit even harder than before, his fingers pulling the folds and stretching them slightly without making me feel any pain.

Pain was what I was already feeling from the way Otis was inside my mouth, pounding in and out of it. Pain, the smell of our sex, and of his come. The smells were almost overwhelming, but that was okay.

"Do you like it when I do this?" The doctor asked, sliding one of his fingers into my hole. My tunnel couldn't resist it, clenching on it like it owned it. Looking down through my legs, I couldn't help but notice the filthy smile on his face.

I nodded, responding, "I love it. Please go on." He widened his smile and slid another of his fingers into my tunnel, this time having to push through the flesh and stretch it. He was thinking about it, wasn't he? He was thinking about penetrating me with his huge, thick shaft, and I was willing to let it happen.

Squeezing my legs together, I urged him to go on. And seeing what was happening, he decided to tap on his friends' backside. The big man groaned, but still jumped off the medical bed. As soon as he was back on his feet on the floor, he started to stroke his massive toy. It was pointing right at me and it was just as red as before. The only difference was that it was also looking a little slicker.

It was thanks to whatever was coming out of the hole in his shaft. Noticing that I was looking down at it, he couldn't hide the smile that appeared on his face. "You want to know what this is?" He asked, taking a step toward me.

I could only nod again. The moment he lowered his head as he bent his body slightly, I knew he was going to grant my wish. "I'm not going to tell you what it is, but I'm going to tell you what it does." His eyes locked with mine, making me feel paralyzed again. "It'll make you pregnant."

My eyes went inside my head, that revelation making me feel

like my life was turning upside down right in front of my eyes. I was so happy that, at the end of this, they were going to get me pregnant.

The nice doctor put another finger inside my hole, moving it left and right, and rubbing it inside of me. Each rub was like sending me to heaven, a word I remembered well right now. Some people I once cared about kept bringing it up, that if I were doing something like this in my life, it wouldn't allow me in.

Well, now was a bit too late for that. Milk coming out of my nipples, my 'boobs' bigger than they'd ever been – and feeling even sorer than before – I knew I'd entered a path I couldn't turn away from.

Otis wrapped his lips around my other nipple, pressing them on it as he drew more and more of my milk out. He was savage and thirsty, wanting all of my milk for himself. It wasn't too long until another wave of orgasm was exploding inside of me, my body convulsing while I felt that nothing more than the Velcro was holding me in place on the medical bed.

Otis nibbled on my earlobe with his milk-coated lips, allowing seconds to pass so that I could return to reality. I felt that the only thing keeping me in here was his lips. They stopped playing with my earlobe all of a sudden, allowing me some time to breathe.

"How was that, honey? Ready for something even more exciting than this?" He asked, putting his hands under me and making me sit up on the medical bed. Turning my eyes down, I realized that the doctor was still with his three fingers inside of me.

The look on his face was telling. He was thinking about what we were going to do together now.

CHAPTER 5

I couldn't believe what was happening to me. I was crawling across the floor, naked like I was before. A collar was around my neck and a leash was connected to it. Feeling the hand of the man tugging at it, he took me to another room in the farmhouse, where he said we were going to do amazing things together.

They painted my skin in white, with dark blotches dotting it. The collar that was around my neck had a small bell connected to it, which jingled every time we moved. And on my skin was a depression that followed the format of the logo of their farm. They branded me. These cowboys – and the doctor – branded me as one of their own.

I could feel their eyes on me, sizing me up. The cowboys were behind me as the doctor took me to that room. I knew it was special the moment I put my hand inside it. Looking from left to right, I couldn't help but think we were going to do things here we would never forget.

"Put her on the table," Walter demanded of Otis, who was eager to obey. He grabbed me with just his arms, hoisting me up. Putting me on the table, he made sure that only my torso, arms, and head were on it. The rest of my body was outside the table, my butt pointing up.

A hand settling on my butt, he started to draw small circles on it. I couldn't turn my head to peek over my shoulder and see who was doing that, but it didn't matter. I knew it was one of the cowboys. The only one that hadn't yet done anything with me was Walter, who was eager to make up for that.

"You really found something special," he growled, moving his finger so that it was touching my other hole. I shivered, feeling his finger a bit too hot right now. There was just something about it that kept drawing me to it, though.

"Am I good enough for you, Master?" I asked him, identifying, through his voice, that he was indeed Walter.

"You're more than that, little angel," he growled again, lowering his body and sticking his tongue out. He flicked it over my hole, making me shiver again. I thought that he was going to take his time, but the sound of his shaft's skin moving up and down told me otherwise. He was already thinking about penetrating me and showing me what having a good time truly was about.

Sweat pooling on my forehead, I couldn't wait until he was doing that for me.

In the meantime, someone was standing right in front of me. It was the nice doctor, his cock pointed at me and eager to enter my mouth. Prying my lips open with his fingers, he did just that after taking a step toward me. I felt his dick stretching my lips, making them wider and going all the way to the back of my throat.

Oh God, it was too much. God didn't like this, though, I thought to myself before realizing that I shouldn't even be thinking about him anymore.

"Do you want me to go on?" Walter asked, blowing his hot air over my ass cheeks. I shivered, feeling like the only thing I wanted right now was to have him pounding in and out of me.

"Yes, Daddy," I answered, shaking my butt so that he knew. He widened his smile, grabbed my hips, and started to penetrate me with his cock. Pain started to shoot through my body, making me arch my back. "Do whatever you want with me."

"That's what I like to hear," he said, yanking me to him. I felt his cock reaching the end of my tunnel, my asshole. Now that I had been living with them for some time, I knew all about those filthy terms. I wasn't shy and naïve anymore, knowing that my life was about just one thing right now – getting pregnant and having their heirs, like all the hucows living on the farm.

He picked up his pace soon after, his fingers digging hard into my skin while drops of sweat pooled under my armpits. When his dick throbbed and his balls tensed up, I knew he was about to come. And come he did, shooting rope after rope of his hot cum inside of me. It took such a toll on him that his lungs were begging for air. He kissed the back of my neck and then pulled out, much to my displeasure. He didn't even finish inside my pussy, which meant that I wasn't going to have his heirs inside my belly. I couldn't believe it!

Moments later, the nice doctor started to pick up his pace after grabbing my head. Pain started to wave through my body as he erupted inside. I wasn't going to deny that his hot and salty cum was still everything I wanted right now, but something was still missing.

They all rounded the table and stopped right behind me. A moment of silence ensued, their minds taking in what they were seeing. "Jesus, she's begging for us to knock her up."

And yes, I was. One after the other, they did me. Pounding hard, in and out of me, they filled me up with their sperm. When they pulled out, it started to dribble and come out. But they were attentive and pushed it back inside me with their fingers, soon walking out of the room and closing the door.

Now that they already knocked me up, I wasn't worth more than a penny to them.

And I wouldn't have it any other way.

The End

Looking for the first 3 books in the series? Download them here:

1. Cowboys' Lucky Age Gap

2. Cowboys' Naughty Age Gap

3. Cowboys' Christmas Age Gap

Lastly, leave a review if you liked this book. It really helps me.

SNEAK PEEK: COWBOYS' LUCKY AGE GAP

Fertile First Time Thanksgiving Story (Hucow Milking Farm - 1)

Perhaps everything would be so much easier if that hunk of a man wasn't seated across from me. We were in the dining room, and I wasn't alone.

His colleague was also with us, picking up a glass of wine and taking a sip from it. His eyes were locked with mine and it was like he was trying to read my mind.

I wasn't trying to read his mind, but I was ogling him without making it obvious I was doing that. I had no idea if he was picking that up, but he smiled and I could see the beautifulness of his super white teeth.

I was just checking him out, wishing I could be in his arms. They looked so strong, confident, veins popping out where I could more easily see them, hair in all the right places, and his skin tanned by the light of the sun. I'd been fantasizing about him since coming here.

And it wasn't just Walter's arms that made my pussy wet, but also his face. And more specifically, his lips.

I wouldn't say that they were big, but they look just right and

I knew that if I were kissing them now, I'd be tasting how sweet they were.

His face was chiseled and looked perfect. He groomed his full, thick beard every day, and it looked sharp without making him look gay.

It gave him that extra spice of manliness I always craved in a man. Looking down slightly, I also loved how his beard transitioned to his neck. I could just imagine myself lying in his bed with him and cradling my head in the crook of his neck. I was pretty sure he would love it if I did that.

But something was impeding me from doing that, and it was the fact that I was a virgin. I didn't know much about these two guys, but I knew that they craved women that had a lot more experience.

I didn't want to disappoint them or myself.

His blond hair seemed to draw my attention to him, and I couldn't control that I was ogling it too. It was short, a bit bigger at the top, and even shorter at the sides. I had no idea if he got his hair cut often, but it was always sharp. This wasn't the first time I was checking him out, after all.

His eyes were icy blue and I suddenly found myself entranced by them. His eyes showed me that behind his tough persona, he was a free-spirited and extroverted man. I didn't need that to tell me that was what he was like, but it was great having that confirmation again.

Seated beside him was his colleague. He was forking a piece of meat on his plate, and I noticed the veins popping out on his forearms. His skin was also white, but just as tanned.

He didn't have a full beard like Walter, but his stubble actually made him look sexier. I could just imagine what it would be like to be grazing my hands over his chin and jawline, feeling the roughness of his skin.

Go to the next page for more books like this one.

BOOKS BY THIS AUTHOR

SERIES - FAVORITE HUCOWS

1. First Time in the Barn: A Fertile Harem Story

2. First Time in the Pen: A Fertile Harem Story

3. First Time in the Shed: A Fertile Harem Story

4. First Time in the Tractor: A Fertile Harem Story

5. First Time on the Haystack: A Fertile Harem Story

SERIES - FERTILE ONLY

1. Bumping the Teacher: A Hucow Mafia First Time Story

2. Bumping the Midwife: A Hucow Mafia First Time Story

3. Bumping the Farmhand: A Hucow Mafia First Time Story

4. Bumping the Sinner: A Hucow Mafia First Time Story

SERIES - HUCOW FOR WHITE COLLARS

1. Milked by the Lawyers: A First Time Bimbo Ménage Story

2. Milked by Doctors: A First Time Bimbo Ménage Story

3. Milked by Engineers: A First Time Bimbo Ménage Story

4. Milked by Directors: A First Time Bimbo Ménage Story

5. Milked by Managers: A First Time Bimbo Ménage Story

And you can also get these fertile hucow mega bundles:

1. Creaming the Bimbo: A Fertile Hucow MEGA Collection

2. Milked by Cowboys: A Hucow Milking MEGA Bundle

3. Milked for Christmas: 15 First Time Hucow Stories

4. Fertile Leakers: 10 Milking Stories

5. Milked, Shared and Used: 16 Stories of Milking Ladies

ABOUT THE AUTHOR

Leandra's Camilli's obsession? Writing dirty, steamy stories that will make you drool. She loves her Alpha males, hucows, sissies, and futas. If you're looking for that kind of book, you've found the right author page.

With a cup of coffee on her table and warm socks on, she writes almost every day. Leandra Camilli's been present in several top 100 categories in the store, and she always finishes her stories.

Made in the USA
Middletown, DE
26 January 2022

59657027R10015